D1823897

"Dodger Dog Meets Shea"

Written by Karen Gee

Illustrations by Kim Wymer

ISBN-13: 978-1537213279

Thank you so much for buying this book, which is number three in the Dodger Dog series.
"Dodger Dog Meets Shea" is the true story of the adoption of Shea, Dodger's sister, as recalled by Dodger himself.
"Dodger Dog Meets Shea" teaches children about adoption and disability, as Shea is a deaf dog.
Find out all about Dodger's mission to help others on his website www.dodgerdog.co.uk

You can also follow Dodger Dog's adventures on Twitter @Ilovedodgerdog

Every Dodger Dog book purchased means that you are helping an animal rescue charity, either in the UK or across the world.

Some of the charities Dodger Dog supports are:

RSPCA
The Dogs Trust
Battersea Dogs & Cats Home
Second Chance Rescue NYC Dogs
I Love Dogs
Soi Dog Foundation

ACKNOWLEDGEMENTS

Karen – My inspiration comes from my love of dogs and passion for helping others. From an early age, dogs were a big part of my life. I firmly believe that every dog deserves to be loved and cherished.

Kim – I was, initially, a cat person. I started painting cats and was a cat owner for many years, until I met Dodger, fell in love with him, and my love of dogs began.

We would both like to thank our families for their love and support. A special thank you to Sinead for her help with getting yet another Dodger Dog into print, and Siobhan for originally bringing Dodger into our lives. We would also like to give a massive thank you to the amazing Dodger Dog Team. You can meet them all on our website www.dodgerdog.co.uk

Dodger Dog

Meets Shea

Long walks on sunny days are great and meeting new friends on these walks makes it even better! I love it when I get to play and I believe that I have lots of fun and adventures because I am such a friendly little dog. I often meet new doggie and human friends when I am out!

One of my favourite games is chasing a ball across the marshes, which is always much better when I have someone else to share and play with! On the days that I don't meet new friends, I always think about how great it would be to have a brother or sister who I can play with *every* day!

It was a warm and sunny day, and it started out pretty much the same as any other. I expected us to go for our usual afternoon walk over the marshes, when suddenly mum said, "Dodger, we are going somewhere special today, we are going for a ride in the car."

We have been to lots of interesting and exciting places in our car, so I was really happy. I jumped into my seat straight away and waited for mum to fasten my seat belt. It seemed like we travelled quite a long way. I looked out of the window and I could see lots of grassy fields, big trees and beautiful flowers; I quickly realised that we were going on an adventure!

As we pulled into the car park, I noticed the place had a familiar feel to it, as though I had been there before! We parked the car, then my lead was attached and I jumped down onto the ground.

'What is this place?' I wondered. 'Why does it feel so familiar?'

We went inside and there were lots of friendly faces, which made my tail wag very fast indeed!

Mummy spoke to one of the ladies and I heard her say, "We are here to meet Holly." 'Fantastic!' I thought. I love to meet new friends and wondered, 'Who is Holly? What is she like, and does she like to play ball?' I was very happy and my tail was wagging! It was going to be a lot of fun – I just knew it!

We were taken through a door and I realised why this place looked and felt so familiar. There were rows and rows of kennels and it looked just like the place where I had stayed as a pup, before I found my forever home. As we walked along, lots of dogs ran out into their play areas and barked, "Hello." I woofed Hello back of course, and wondered if Holly lived here.

We stopped at a kennel, where a kennel maid greeted us and told us to wait right there. Then she returned with a beautiful white and black dog on a lead. 'So, this is Holly,' I thought as I said, "Hello." As we walked along to a fenced play area, I introduced myself to Holly with some friendly barks, told her my name and started to ask her questions about herself.

Holly didn't reply! 'That's rude,' I thought. 'Maybe she's just shy?' So, I decided to be really friendly and see what fun we could have together. The gate was open and as we walked into the play area I noticed a football on the grass. 'This is going to be great,' I thought, 'we are going to have fun here'. We both had our leads removed and I ran to get the football.

Friendly dogs always share, so I decided to take it in turns to hold the ball, I ran over to Holly and dropped the ball at her feet. "Thank you!" she woofed. This was the first time Holly spoke to me!   After that we ran, sharing the football and having fun! We barked and chatted, then Holly told me her story, about how she had ended up living in the animal rescue centre.

Holly told me she was deaf. She explained that when I had spoken to her earlier she wasn't being rude or ignoring me, she just couldn't hear me! I was relieved, as I really liked Holly and wanted us to become friends. Holly explained she understood me now that we were face to face, as she could read my barks and understand my signs and body language.

This was very new to me, I had never met a deaf dog before. It started me thinking about other dogs and people that I had met on my walks. Sometimes I barked and got no response, so maybe they were deaf too? It was so good that Holly taught me how I could communicate with her. We carried on playing and it was much more fun for both of us because we could understand each other.

After a while, mummy put our leads back on and told us it was time to go. We said our goodbyes, but I didn't really like leaving my new friend at the kennels. As we made our way back to the car I had my sad face on, but I smiled when mummy told me we would come and visit Holly another day. Then she told me what a good boy I had been that day, which made me very happy!

Later that week we went to play with Holly again at the kennels. We had such a great time together, running around playing ball and rough-and-tumble on the grass! Holly told me stories about some of her friends and how they had found their forever homes, like me, and I told her that one day so would she! I was surprised by what Holly told me next …

This was not the first time that Holly had lived here. When she was a tiny puppy, she was brought here with her mum and her brothers and sisters. When they were old enough, the puppies started to get visitors and one by one they all found their forever homes. Holly said it was strange living in a house, not at all like living in the kennels with her family, and she missed them.

The family that rescued Holly used to go out quite a lot and leave her alone in the house. Being a young pup, she soon became bored, so she began to find mischief when they were gone! Chewing things was a great way to have some fun when she was left alone!

They also found it difficult to communicate with her and this is when it was first discovered that Holly was deaf.

Eventually, the family decided that they didn't have the time or patience needed to care for a puppy, especially one with special needs like Holly, so they took her back to the kennels. When she arrived her family had all gone to their new homes, and she was left alone in her kennel, feeling very lonely and missing them lots and lots.

During the previous three months other families had come to see Holly and taken her out for walks, however, when they found out that she was deaf, they decided to choose a different dog to take home with them. I was shocked to find out that sometimes people decide to take their dogs back to the kennels and I couldn't understand this at all!

It was a Saturday and I can remember it extremely well. Mum got me up early and I had my breakfast. Then she said to me, "Dodger, today is a very special day. We are going to see Holly and bring her home to live with us." I could not believe my ears! I was so happy! I was sure Holly didn't know about this, my tail started to wag and I ran around barking very excitedly!

When we arrived at the rescue centre mum had to sit down and fill in the adoption papers before we could take Holly with us.

Then we walked down to the kennels where she was waiting. Lots of people walk dogs at the rescue centre, so us visiting again didn't seem unusual to Holly. I woofed, "Hello," and we went for our usual walk.

We played in the sun happily and when it was time to leave, instead of going to the kennel, we carried on to our car! I smiled, and Holly looked at me with a very excited look on her face. Then Mum stopped and told us, "Holly is coming home with us, she will be your new sister and we will call her Shea. You will need to look after Shea, Dodger." New adventures are about to begin!

The End!

Others in the series:

How I Became Dodger Dog!

Dodger Dog's Muddy Mistake

Coming soon:

Dodger Dog's Christmas Message

Dodger Dog Learns Something New

Dodger Dog at the Caravan

Dodger Dog Finds a Job

Find out more about Dodger's mission to help others on his website:

www.dodgerdog.co.uk

Also follow Dodger's antics on Twitter, Facebook & Instagram:

@ I Love Dodger Dog

Join Dodger's free club on his website:

"I love Dodger Dog club"